THE PALE WHITE

CHAD LUTZKE

Published by Crystal Lake Publishing
Where Stories Come Alive!

Crystal Lake Publishing
www.CrystalLakePub.com

**Follow us on
Amazon:**

WELCOME
TO ANOTHER

CRYSTAL LAKE PUBLISHING
CREATION

Join today at www.crystallakepub.com & www.patreon.com/CLP

OTHER WORKS BY CHAD LUTZKE:

Novellas:
Of Foster Homes and Flies
Wallflower
Stirring the Sheets
Skullface Boy
Out Behind the Barn
The Same Deep Water as You

Collections:
Night as a Catalyst (Revised & Expanded)
Spicy Constellation & Other Recipes

OTHER NOVELLAS BY CRYSTAL LAKE PUBLISHING

A Season in Hell by Kenneth W. Cain
Quiet Places: A Novella of Cosmic Folk Horror by Jasper Bark
The Final Reconciliation by Todd Keisling
Devourer of Souls by Kevin Lucia
Apocalyptic Montessa and Nuclear Lulu: A Tale of Atomic Love by Mercedes M. Yardley
Little Dead Red by Mercedes M. Yardley

Or check out other Crystal Lake Publishing books for more Tales from the Darkest Depths.

Dedicated to the abused and neglected. No matter the degree.
And for the girls.

CHAPTER 1

IT'S BEEN DARK for an hour and I'm the first one up. Usually am. I stare at the ceiling and pretend I'm somewhere else, pretend it's all been a dream. It took about a week to get used to staying up all night, sleeping all day. We rarely get to bed before noon. That's Doc's doing. Nobody wants to rape a girl in broad daylight, the sun spotlighting their sin.

I turn on the lamp next to my bed and look over at the top of the stairs, where Doc puts our food. The same empty plates sit there, stacked and licked clean. It's been like this for days. Not a crumb in sight. Being hungry is one thing, but when food is the highlight of your day, the days slow down and stretch into something tortuous, maddening. If it weren't for Alex and Kammie, I'd have taken a broken bulb to my wrist months ago.

Doc is punishing us. Alex had bitten a guy's neck. The guy went to Doc, demanded his money back, bitching about what the hell is he gonna tell his wife about the marks on his neck. He doesn't know how lucky he is she didn't rip his throat out. Not that she's done it before, but she would. She'd love to.

"You asshole!" I yell. It wakes Alex, stirs Kammie.

Alex peeks at the stairs with a makeup-filled eye, sees the empty plates. She kicks off the bed sheets in a fit, lets out a little whine. She's still in her fishnets. Of the three of us, she's the only one who doesn't mind the clothes Doc gives her. The black skirts, the leather, the Bettie Page bangs. Everything is black, goth and punk and speaks volumes about her rebelliousness. Her punk rock mentality. Whether the anarchist in her is from something else or brought on by too many years under Doc's thumb, I don't know. But it fits, and I envy it.

I look at Kammie. Her back is to us, her finger tracing something on the wall. Probably a flower. It's all she ever draws. Her nightgown is covered in them. So are her sheets, drawn in multi-colored markers. I think she does it to remind herself she's a girl. Doc dresses her as a boy, her hair kept short. She has no figure yet, not at nine. And it pacifies the clients looking for a young boy, but without feeling gay. I guess that little detail helps them sleep at night.

I head down the attic stairs with weak legs and stand on the bottom step. The door is locked. Always. I hit the door with the flat of my hand. "Let's go, Doc! We get it, alright!?"

I listen. Nothing. I head back upstairs.

Alex is sitting on the bed, lacing her boots. "This shit stops now," she says. "What we've always talked about doing but never have? We're doing it. The second Doc shows his face."

She's talking about killing him.

Kammie sticks her thumb in her mouth and looks through the barred window at the beach below. The moon licks the incoming waves. Stars on a black liquid canvas. It's a million miles away. She rocks on her heels, knees bent to her chin. Her nightgown is stretched tight, hiding her pencil legs. She hasn't said a word since I've been here. Alex said she used to talk, too much even. But when Doc was ready to use her, she never spoke again. Alex said the last words she ever said were, "I love you, too," as she was led out of the room, holding Doc's hand. Alex's pillowcase is covered with the stain of mascara and eyeliner from that night. She said she's never cried so much in her life. And now Kammie spends her time near the window with her fern, a potted plant.

"Maybe he's not coming back," I say. "Maybe he's done with us."

"No. He's pulled this shit before. You weren't here yet."

"He starved you guys?"

"No, just me."

"What'd you do?"

"Scratched the shit out of somebody. He was tearing me up, Stac."

I don't know what to say. I've only been here a year, been through my own hell. But not like Alex. Not like Kammie.

I stare at the shag carpet in our room. Dark yellow and matted, stained where I vomited once. It was my first time and a client made me drink too much wine. I was a virgin until that night.

I hate calling them clients. The word gives a false perception that I willingly provide a service. I have no will here. They're not my clients. They're Doc's. They're my demons, my living scars, my bane, and the subject of every murderous thought I have.

"I'm worried about Kam," I say.

"She'll be fine once we're outta here."

The room feels claustrophobic, something I thought I'd get used to but haven't. There's a single window in the room, covered by bars. Behind the bars is plexiglass painted white, with little scratches in the paint. Kammie did it with her fingernail, scratching in a flower with petals you can look through and see the beach. Alex said there used to be three other windows, but Doc covered them years ago with brick, then drywall.

Alex eyes the room. I know she's looking for a weapon. She really does mean to kill him. The room is empty of all but books, our beds, and two small lamps. We have no dressers. No closets. When a change of clothes is needed, Doc brings them up based on the client's preference. School girl uniforms being the most popular for me, sometimes an elegant gown when Doc tries to lady me up. I don't look seventeen when I'm done up and in those dresses. I guess that's the idea.

"What if we don't kill him? What if we just break out?" I ask.

Murder. Other than daydreaming about it, I don't think I have it in me. Even under the circumstances.

"What the hell, Stacia? If we could do that, I would have done it ten years ago."

"I can't kill someone."

"Doc's a piece of shit. He deserves it. Besides, it's what vampires do."

That's her thing. Vampires. In some twisted way I think that's how she copes, pretending to have blood lust, avoiding sunlight, immortality. All that. I let her carry on with the facade. Never argued with her over it. If it keeps her from losing her shit, slicing her wrists, so be it.

"Get your shoes."

I look at my side of the room. There are two pairs of high heels in the corner. One red, one black. It's all I have. Alex sees them.

"Never mind," she says. "Come on." She grabs my hand and heads for the stairs. "We'll get him up here, then I'll push him down the stairs. With any luck, the asshole will break his neck."

I look at the stairs. They're steep, wooden. If he falls, he's not getting back up. We head down the stairs. Alex sits on the bottom step and pats it, inviting me next to her.

"We'll sit here and kick the door."

"No way we can break it down."

"We just need his attention. At the count of three, kick it with both feet, like this." Alex rests her arms on the stair behind her, grips it, then lifts her legs. "Ready? One . . . two . . . *three!*"

I'm fatigued from no food, and my barefooted kick is weak against the door. But Alex's boots make up the difference, and the kick thunders through the house. The step behind me is hard against my back, and I feel it on my spine. I've lost more weight, I can tell.

"Doc! Something's wrong with Kammie! She's having a seizure!" Alex screams, kicks the door again. Then we run up the stairs and wait at the top.

"Hold on." Alex says. She runs and fetches one of the lamps. "If he doesn't fall, swing this at his head."

She hands me the lamp. The murder weapon.

"Got it?"

I nod and put the lamp behind my back.

We can hear the pound of Doc's feet heading up to the second floor and toward the attic door, then keys. The door has four separate locks. We've counted, hoping one day he'd forget to lock them. But Doc is too careful.

The sound of each lock opening is barbed wire in my stomach. Alex grinds her teeth.

The door opens.

Doc stands there in his silk pajamas, burgundy. They barely fit him and shimmer in the hallway light. A bloated kidney bean dipped in oil. His hair is slicked back against his giant head, a gun at his side. He never comes up without it. He points it at us and says, "What the hell is goin' on?"

"Hurry! She's dying!" Alex yells.

He heads up the attic stairs, never taking his eyes off us. Gun pointed. The stairs scream under his weight. Doc is huge. I'm guessing 350. If Alex means to push him, she'll have to shove hard. I don't think she can do it. She can't be more than 110 herself. He'll shove back and fire the gun. This is a bad idea.

"What in God's name?" He's winded, holding tight to the handrail. I can hear Alex breathing heavier. She's growling, quietly. Doc nears the top, and Alex's growl escalates into a full shriek. She lunges for him. A feral cat onto an unsuspecting dog. She wraps her legs around him and the gun goes off. The bullet hits the wall behind me, and Alex buries her face in Doc's thick neck, ripping at his throat. Her thumbs find the new wound and split the fat skin, widening the gouge.

I scream for her to stop, not really meaning it.

Kammie runs to me, holding the fern against her chest, her thumb in mouth.

Doc howls as blood sprays the walls, sprays us. His knees buckle and he drops, tumbling down the steps and taking Alex with him. I drop the lamp and scream for Alex. Doc's huge body rolls over her, crushing her against the steps. But she holds on and is on top of him by the time they land. He's not moving anymore, other than the jiggle of his cheeks as she pulls the flesh from his neck with her teeth. It's savage. Animalistic. And I hold Kammie against me, shielding her eyes and covering her ears, while Alex drinks from the man's neck.

CHAPTER 2

"ALEX!" SHE DOESN'T STOP. I can't watch, so I turn away. But I can hear it. It's loud and messy, and unnatural. "Alex!" Finally, she stops. She looks at me, sees me holding Kammie. Her eyes go from rage to confusion. Then she gags and vomits blood down the front of her shirt.

We lock eyes and neither of us are sure what to say. The door to freedom stands open with a gore-filled mess blocking the exit. It's an image impossible to erase. Add it to the rest of them. Freedom or not, it feels like I'll never smile again.

There's silence, and none of us move. None of us spring for the door, run down the street screaming for help. Is this shock? Or is it mourning? And for what? The sack of shit that lay butchered at the bottom of the stairs? Or for our innocence?

Alex wipes her face with the back of her hand, a crimson smile across pale skin. Skin that hasn't seen the sun in years. I don't realize just how bad we look until I see the contrast spread across her face. I look at my own ivory flesh. My legs, my arms. Bleached by malnutrition and a schedule nocturnal.

"Well, there's the door," Alex says.

The three of us stare at the doorway. A gaping maw that feels like a trap. The thought of freedom brings no comfort, and I'm not sure why. I've hated life for the past year, hated my mother for not finding me, hated myself even for allowing countless men to have their way with me, feeding fetishes I never knew existed. But here we are, unmoving. Scared and confused.

Are we beyond rescue? I feel tainted, like the world isn't ready for us, or maybe doesn't want us, and we're not ready for it. But we're not alone. We're sisters. No, the bond is stronger. We're The Pale White. And there's nothing we wouldn't do for one another.

Beyond that door, eventually we'll be separated. Torn apart by authority. Kammie in foster care, Alex on the street with nowhere to run, and me at home with my alcoholic mother and her white-trash boyfriend. I picture myself at home in my bedroom, suffering alone with my trauma, my mother offering me half-assed well wishes in between drinks, as she realizes there's nothing she can do to save me. I'm alone. No Kammie. No Alex. Just the memories of this house on the beach. And I realize in this moment, I don't want to go home. Not if it means leaving them.

I look at Kammie. She's shaking, her eyes fixed on the mess at the bottom of the stairs, waiting for instruction. Trusting us.

I need to take charge, make some kind of call. The first move. "We need clothes."

CHAPTER 3

I HEAD BACK to our room, look around. There's nothing here we'll ever need. I'm not wearing the heels, and I sure as hell am not wearing the school girl uniform, groped and stained by old, pathetic men.

I grab Kammie's hand and we take the stairs. Doc's legs cover the last few steps. I think of the movies with the killer at the end you think is dead, until he reaches for a leg and murders once more. But Doc's not getting up again. There is no life there. His blood has left him, drank by Alex, then regurgitated.

Alex goes through the doorway and we follow, carefully stepping over Doc's body when all I really want to do is walk on it, stomp on his face, and be a part of his suffering, his pain. But his suffering is over, far too quickly.

As we walk through the threshold of the attic door, I wait for the sound of alarms, the charging of perverted old men shoving us back to the attic to be held for further use. But the hall is quiet. Just the whisper of wind tossing rain upon the windows. Windows we can see through.

The hall is dark, the moon barely teasing blue-gray beams across the floor like an old hag's teeth. I know this hall. We're led down here, blindfolded. The second story acting as a brothel, the attic a prison. For the very first time, I'm looking at the closed doors that line the hall. Beyond them I've been through unspeakable things, used to satiate lustful appetites. I have the cracks in each ceiling memorized; the spider in the corner of the room on the left I'd even given a name. Charlotte, after the book. I remember willing her to bite the man who had me the day I named her. Or weaving me a single word of hope within her web that all would be well, that this was almost over and I would be saved. The next day she was gone, the web left empty. And from then on, the web was a constant reminder there was no hope. Even Charlotte hid from the atrocities in that room.

Alex runs back to Doc's body and grabs the gun. She rips his shirt open and his belly jiggles. I've seen that belly too many times, the giant gut pressed against me, stopping the rest of him from getting too close, going too deep. She uses the shirt to wipe the gun free of blood, then grips the gun tight, looks it over, holds it at her side. She's ready to pull the trigger. I feel safer now. Alex will shoot anything that moves.

As far as we know, Doc lived alone, but we creep down the hall like burglars in the night, being careful not to make the slightest noise. I look back at Doc, at his neck. And I almost smile. Almost. I don't know what stops me. The thought of not quite reaching freedom? Or of what kind of sick bitch gives a grin to another person's death? I struggle with those thoughts for a moment and decide the world is a better place without him, then follow Alex down to the first floor, Kammie's hand in mine.

CHAPTER 4

WE'VE NEVER SEEN this part of the house before, and I'm a little taken back by the decor. Victorian in every way, though the house itself is modern. Red velvet drapes cover enormous bay windows. Dark wood throughout, intricately carved along the bannister, accenting chairs, doorways and alcoves. Ceiling-high shelves line the walls stocked with books and beautiful stained glass nestled snug into the front door. Our exit.

The house is not what I expected. Mid-century furniture stained with grime, burned with cigarettes, and littered with molding TV dinners made for an easier assumption considering the kind of monster Doc was.

Was.

It all feels like an extravagant waiting room for the clients, while they choose their flesh from menus filled with enticing photos of young girls in various outfits, striking mannequin-esque poses behind teary eyes. There were photos, plenty of them. Somewhere. And my first inclination was to burn this whole house down. Every outfit. Every photo. Every stained sheet, with Doc the bubbling mass at its center. A marshmallow engulfed. But instead we head straight for the kitchen. We're starving.

Alex flicks the kitchen light on, and the room explodes with fluorescent brilliance. A stark contrast from the dark, gothic room behind us. The floor is checkerboard-tile, the counters black marble, and the appliances stainless steel and near industrial in size. The room is from another era altogether. The bright light hurts our eyes and I wonder if Alex will start her vampire shit again, claiming our sensitivity to such light is secondary to being creatures of the night.

The kitchen looks wholesome and clean, scientific laboratory clean. Hospital clean.

Alex washes her face and hands in the sink, drinks from the faucet, takes her shirt off and wipes the blood from her neck. I'm reminded of my own braless self and wonder if Alex has ever worn one outside of client-specific lingerie. I can't picture her in one, even being out of the house. She's a free spirit, with reckless abandon. Rebellious and full of angst. It's amazing Doc was able to tame her. If she does ever wear a bra, it will be black. That will never change.

We gather at the fridge, our empty stomachs trumping the desire to flee. Or maybe we all know that beyond the front door, we go our separate ways. The fridge is stocked with all kinds of food. None of us take the time to cook. We make sandwiches. Deli. There's leftover Chinese as well as pizza, but we don't touch it. If I had to guess why, I'd say because Doc has already touched it, tainted it with his grimy hands and mouth. No thank you.

I watch Kammie as she struggles to make her own sandwich, and I think about all the food she's never had. Her whole life she's lived off soup, noodles, PB & J, and oatmeal, though one time a client gave her cherries. She'd gotten them all over her bibs and Doc pissed a bitch, yelling at her that clothes cost money and next time he'd make sure she worked it off. I'm not sure what that meant, but if it meant getting the hell out of that attic and scrubbing the floors of another room, or even the toilets, I would have bled through my pants on the regular if I knew it'd cause a "punishment" that could break the monotony of seeing the same walls every hour I'm awake.

I rummage through the cupboards and find a bag of potato chips, several actually. I rip one open and pour some on the counter. "Try these, Kam. They're chips. You can even put them in your sandwich if you want."

"Hot damn!" Alex says. "Where'd you find those? Are there Doritos?"

I show her the cupboard. There are four bags of Doritos, every one of them unopened. A few of them are flavors I know Alex has never had. Those that came out in the last decade. Doc has had food like this in the house the entire time, here in this beautiful home, while he fed us the same thing every day. I'm glad he's dead, that Alex killed him. Does that make me a bad person?

Kammie picks up a chip and tastes it, then grabs a handful and puts them in her sandwich. Seeing this makes me want to cry. Eating potato chips for the very first time should never be a milestone for a nine-year-old. She takes her sandwich and sits at the window in the living room and watches the beach. Alex and I follow and eat in silence as we pace, keeping clear of the scarlet tracks we'd made—quiet steps from the kitchen to the living room and back again. And again. Eyes on the windows, on the doorknobs, waiting for them to turn. It doesn't feel safe, and we eat ravenously. Both out of paranoia and starvation. Mice eating cheese at the foot of a trap.

I pour us glasses of water and they go down fast. More sandwiches are made, chips eaten. It feels strange to not be talking, but it feels like there's nothing to say. I always pictured the three of us exploding through the door, tears of joy, running into the arms of those who can save us. Those who can somehow erase the past and make it all better. But it's not like that.

CHAPTER 5

"CAT." ALEX POINTED at the Siamese in the children's book. "They go, meeoow."

"Meeoow," Kammie mimicked.

"This is a dog. They bark, like this . . . ruff, ruff."

Kammie smiled. Dogs sounded funny. The children's books weren't any kind of charity from Doc. He wasn't into being merciful. They were part of the process. The investment. He couldn't afford for the guilty conscious of a client to get the best of him, to suddenly question his morals in the middle of a transaction with a girl as primitive as Kammie. So, Doc needed her to learn the basics. Alex teaching Kammie was for his benefit, and Alex didn't mind. It passed the time, filled the days with memories worth remembering. It felt good to help Kammie feel adequate, less alone. So, identifying colors, letters, and objects came first. Basic reading would come later.

"Do this one again." Kammie pointed to the pig. It was her favorite because Alex incorporated a funny face along with the noise.

"Oink, oink."

Kammie giggled and Alex took to tickling her.

Then Doc walked in. He hadn't started with the gun yet. That would come later, when Alex was older, more resistant.

"You're playing innocent and naive tonight." Doc threw a stuffed paper bag onto Alex's bed. "Make sure you're shaved. You've got half an hour."

Alex smiled at Kammie behind gritted teeth and stubborn tears, hiding the hell inside.

Doc turned to leave, turned back. "And pigtails . . . half an hour." Then he headed downstairs.

The air fell somber quiet. Kammie closed the book. "When you come back tonight, I'll read to you. I mean . . . I'll try," Kammie said, then wrapped her frail arms around Alex, squeezing hard.

Alex buried her face in Kammie's hair and wet it with a single tear.

CHAPTER 6

"I NEED A SHIRT," **Alex says.**

We leave the living room in search of clothes and keep to the bottom floor of the house. I don't think any of us want to go near the scene at the bottom of the attic stairs. The first room we enter is an office. A large desk in the center sporting a lamp, a computer, and a small stack of books and magazines that shine glossy under the light. Magazines with covers that show too much skin.

There are twice as many books in the office than the living room, and I'm surprised at the amount of them. I pictured Doc more of a porn-all-day kind of guy. One who only let go of his pecker long enough to have his way with one of us or take money from a man just as disgusting as himself.

Then I see a set of shelves lined with DVD cases—all named and numbered. I know what's on them—our innocence being stripped away. Peeled away like so much skin. Another reason to burn it all down.

I turn on the computer. I think I'm the only one who knows what it is until Alex says "This isn't the time for games. We've got shit to do." I try explaining the Internet to her. Something that had never come up in conversation before. My guess is the Internet has played a major role in our being here, whether by email or through a website buried deep—the flesh menu on display for those with access. The screen comes on and asks for a password. I don't even try. It's a waste of time. This isn't a movie, where a hero does the impossible.

"Do you think everyone's address is in there?" Alex asks.

"Probably not. But a list of clients, sure."

"Too bad. We could go on a killing spree." She says it so calmly, like we'd be collecting simple debts for fundraising cookies. "Then I could feed."

CHAPTER 7

WE FINALLY END up on the second floor again. The attic door remains open, and we all avoid looking. Even Alex. But I can feel Doc's dead eyes peering at me through the gap in the door, and I hold my breath as we pass.

We find a closet at the end of the hallway. It's filled with clothes. Most we recognize, some we don't. We grab those. Alex takes a black T-shirt with lips and a tongue on it and smiles when she sees it. "My mother loved the Stones," she says, then puts on the shirt. It's an old, familiar skin.

Kammie finds a nice dress that fits her. It's yellow and white. She puts it on and looks so beautiful, and I tell her so. Her mouth gives the weakest little smile. A forced thing that is afraid to show itself.

I look for jeans and find none. Clients aren't turned on by denim. It doesn't reveal. It doesn't lift with the flick of a Rolex-covered wrist. And it doesn't tear. Instead, I find slacks, black. These are for that business-woman look, complete with messy bun and glasses. I find the white blouse that matches and put it on. It'll do for now.

At the bottom of the closet are shoes, nearly all of

them are heels. There are boy's tennis shoes that fit Kammie. She picks a pair and puts them on. I finally find a pair of saddle shoes. Schoolgirl uniform shit. Alex has her boots.

We head over to a tall mirror mounted on the wall. And it's the first time in so very long that the person looking back almost feels like me. Instead of making sure I look arousable—per Doc's instructions—I'm searching for the old me, begging her to still be there, somewhere.

Kammie seems the most content and even spins in front of the mirror, watching the hypnotic motion of her dress as it rises and falls. She looks so beautiful.

I look at Alex. She's got her fist pressed against the mirror, a punk-rock snarl with her upper lip.

"I'm damaged," she says.

She's right. We all are.

CHAPTER 8

Alex closed the book after reading the last page. It was her fourth book so far that week, the only thing that kept her from shutting down, other than Kammie. She questioned why Doc only allowed books with a dark theme. Were they the only books he had? Or was this his idea of mental manipulation? Offering bleak, post-apocalyptic tales and stories of murder, monsters, cosmic horror, and vampires. Vampires being Alex's favorite. Normal people having been turned into attractive, immortal beings with a penchant for blood. Was this Doc's way of creating his own monster? Or was it much simpler than that and these were the only books he owned? Too lazy to go to the library but having just enough sympathy to offer something to pass the time, taking little effort to choose a book and grabbing the first that caught his eye.

Despite the morbid subject matter of each book, Alex found solace in them and knew if what the books offered were love stories with happy endings, lessons on joyful living, or those that offered hope in a world that didn't exist, those would be the books that would tear her down. Somehow the dark nature of a *humanoid creature of the night ending the life of another gave her more hope than anything.*

And in between stories, in between coddling Kammie, teaching her, and reading to her from the children's books, in between hours where she lies on a bed with a hell-bound man, she daydreamed of killing Doc. And there she found hope.

CHAPTER 9

"COME HERE, GUYS," Alex says. She heads to the living room where she sits on a large couch, her legs Indian style. She waits for us to sit down, then looks us each in the eyes.

Kammie has brought her fern and strokes the leaves, the feel of them calming her.

"What do you think about staying here for a while? Until we get shit figured out."

Kammie looks out the window, lost in the beach again.

"Why would we do that?" I ask. But I know why.

"Do you really want to go home? Back to your drunk mother, to her asshole boyfriend? What does he call you? Hot stuff?"

"Maybe she's changed. What if me missing scared her straight?"

"You really believe that?"

I gaze at the floor, wounded. "And if someone comes to the door? What then?"

"We don't answer. Simple as that."

But it isn't that simple. There must be a hundred things we aren't considering. I look at Kammie, disinterested and lost, or unable to make a decision on her own, waiting for us to lead the way. I think about how she'd feel if she knew what would happen to The Pale White beyond that stained-glass door. The separation. The solitude. If she knew, if she had any idea, then she'd offer pleading eyes not to go. Not now. Maybe she'd even speak. Shout her disagreement and state her argument.

I decide that maybe it's best to give ourselves time to think, just for a day or two, and then I ask Alex if she still has the gun. She pulls it out from the back of her skirt and shows me.

"Okay, keep it. And if someone else gets in the house other than us . . . shoot them." I can't believe I said it. I can't believe we're staying.

CHAPTER 10

*I*T WAS MOTHER'S DAY. *Stacia and her mother had fought all weekend. A normal routine, but not to this extent. Slaps had been thrown, hair pulled, and a lengthy grounding issued out of spite. This wasn't the usual drunken fog. This came from the problem with James, the live-in boyfriend for the past eighteen months. Their relationship had hit a rather turbulent storm because of strip-bar allegations. More specifically, a lap dance that ended with a spent James and a heavy tip. A tip meant for groceries and the electric bill.*

Friday and Saturday were spent with intermittent screaming fits between the dysfunctional couple, flying dishes, and fists through walls—calmed only by a visit from local law enforcement. Saturday evening, however, was filled with makeup sex. Exaggeratingly loud, drunken and everlasting. If it weren't for headphones, Stacia would have run away that very night, embarrassed, sickened, and bitter.

After Stacia's father died when she was a toddler, her mother took to the bottle, the problem growing worse over the years and hitting a peak over the past two, James heavily contributing to this second level of hell. The constant fighting was exhausting, particularly for Stacia, as she was the only one who could recollect every poisonous word said the night before, her mother often waking as if nothing ever happened.

On Sunday, Stacia pretended to do the same. It was a difficult attempt at loving unconditionally. Looking past the alcoholism, past the neglect, the emotional and physical abuse, the ease her mother seemed to have with neglecting her for James. And Mark. And Brian—a never-ending chain of codependency.

Stacia took extra care with the bacon. Not too crisp, not too soggy. She made omelets with cheese, peppers, and mushrooms, then buttered toast and arranged it all on a tray and carried it to her mother's room with a glass of OJ filled to the top and threatening to spill with each step.

The gesture took everything she had as she maneuvered the obstacle that was the hallway—dirty laundry, empty bottles of beer, a litter box far too full of dung, and a stack of books her mom would never read but always meant to. With each step closer to the bedroom door, there was reluctance. Her mother didn't deserve this olive branch.

The door was cracked open. Stacia pushed it further with her elbow. The room was trashed, littered with much of the same found in the hall, along with dishes stabbed with cigarette butts. The walls were covered in tapestries sporting eagles, skulls, and motorcycles. The room resembled a bachelor pad for a derelict chauvinist, not the bedroom of a mother in her 40s. The entire house had been overcome with such decor once James moved in. *Harley Davidson swag, American flags, Anheuser-Busch and even a six-foot cardboard standee of a large-breasted woman in a pink bikini nailed to the living room wall.*

Nothing had the touch of a woman anymore. Nothing at all reflected the proud mother Stacia had seen in her baby pictures—evidence that at one time Deborah Squires was someone else entirely. Someone full of life and love to give.

Stacia prepared a plastic smile and stepped into the room. It reeked of alcohol-soaked tongues and the skunk of cigarette butts. She focused on the floor, watching her step. Dodging, maneuvering, until she was at the foot of the bed, then looked up at her mother and James.

They were sprawled naked, James still sporting the shriveled condom from the night before. It had been a horrible idea, breakfast in bed. She turned and left the room, the image of the two stuck behind her eyes like black spots from the sun.

She bent down and fed the olive branch to the dog.

CHAPTER 11

I TURN ON the TV and find cartoons for Kammie. She's entranced and smiling, and it's the best thing I've seen in a year. I sit next to Alex who's got Doc's Rolodex in her lap, flipping through it. I know what she's doing. Looking for them. The pedophiles with wives at home who don't know any better.

"Nothing will come of that," I say. "You know these guys never give out their names . . . not to us. Most of those people in there are family and friends . . . completely innocent."

"One gave me his name. That asshole thought he was in love with me. Told me all kinds of shit. Talked about his kids, how his wife hates him because he won't buy her a new tub because the old one's just fine. His name was Richard . . . Dick." She laughs and keeps flipping through the names.

"And if you find him in there what are you gonna do?"

"Nothing anymore. There's three Richards in here so far."

"And if there weren't?

"Not sure. Call his wife. Maybe lure him here."

"Lure him here?"

"To feed."

I pull Alex into the kitchen so Kammie can't hear us. "Will you please stop it with the bloodsucking shit?"

"I don't expect you to understand, Stac. Apparently, Doc never turned you."

"Alex, he never turned you either. This used to be cute and I've always played along, but now it's time to wake up. We're free. We should be getting the hell out of here."

"First of all, what went on behind closed doors hasn't been the same for all of us. You know what I'm saying? You don't know what Doc did to me, what he did to Kammie. Look at her! She looks like a boy!"

I hold my hand up to quiet Alex and peek out at Kammie. She's still fixed on the TV.

"She looks beautiful. Don't say that again."

"What I'm saying is, every one of us was being groomed for this. To become vampires and do Doc's bidding. The lack of sunlight, the letting of blood . . . "

"What letting of blood?"

"This is exactly what I mean. Different experiences behind closed doors."

"What are you talking about?"

"This couple. They liked blood stuff. She'd come in on her period and . . . " Alex stopped. She didn't explain further, and I didn't push her. These are scars that are supposed to be healing, not re-opened.

At this point, I become more worried about Alex than Kammie and decide that despite the fear of losing one another, this is not a safe place. This is not a good idea. The memories here provide no healing. They poke and prod and cloud judgment. They violate our nose in the form of bleached linen, our ears with the distant crashing of waves and the creaking of wooden stairs, and our psyches with the ghosts of our innocence. The house feels haunted with a presence that would never allow for moving on, and we need to get out. I start to explain this to Alex, when I'm interrupted by a loud knock at the door.

CHAPTER 12

STACIA SAT ON the couch at the party just blocks from her house. She was uncomfortable. She knew there would probably be beer, maybe even a few of the kids in the back bedroom passing a joint. But not cocaine. Not pills.

Even on the coffee table in front of her, classmates were deflowering their noses with the powder, rolled dollar bills and lines cut by driver's licenses they didn't deserve. She was watching the downfall of young potential, and it sickened her. She broke a sweat and wiped her clammy hands on her jeans. She would be leaving soon. It was a matter of finding the courage, or a believable excuse. In the meantime, she would watch the cocaine disappear into healthy, naive faces.

If she left now, right in the middle of this, she would hear about it at school, about what a chickenshit she was. Acceptance was important to her, but not at this cost. She refused to turn out like her mother, living in a bottle, settling for men with nothing to offer.

She held a large cup of beer in her hand, one that she had no real intention of drinking, but did anyway.

This wasn't becoming her mother. This was coping. This was surviving high school. Kids can be cruel.

Kenny Jarvis, a boy she'd crushed on for as long as she could remember, offered her a line that was cut on the table only two feet in front of her. It would take all the effort of bending over.

"No thanks . . . I like my beer," she tipped the cup to her mouth and didn't stop drinking until he looked away. Those beautiful eyes of his.

Before the evening was through, Stacia would end up in the back bedroom, stripped naked and drugged unconscious.

CHAPTER 13

THE KNOCK AT the door is gunshot loud. Kammie runs to Alex and hides behind her. I look at the clock. It's 11:00 p.m. A voice interrupts the knocking. "Come on, Doc! Cash in hand. You said tonight. Let's go!"

I think we're just going to ignore the guy, and then Alex pushes Kammie gently to me and pulls the gun from her waistband, heads for the door. I whisper not to, but her hand is on the knob and she's looking through the stained glass.

"I know this one," she whispers.

Her words scare me. I know what she's thinking— this is an opportunity.

I whisper-shout for her to get away from the door. "Alex! You said we wouldn't answer it."

She looks back at me, and her grip on the doorknob tightens.

"Please don't."

The look she gives me says "I'm sorry." Then she opens the door.

A man stands on the porch wearing a dress shirt with a tie, a briefcase in hand. Anywhere else he'd look like a salesman, maybe a Jehovah's Witness. His fist is held up, mid knock. He goes wide-eyed at the sight of Alex, and the gun pointed at him.

"Get in the house."

"Where's Doc?"

"He's upstairs," she says.

The guy looks at me, sees me holding Kammie, sees the look on my face, looks back at Alex.

"I said get in the house!"

"Or what?"

"Do you not see this gun, dickhead?"

"You won't shoot me."

"Are you dumb enough to find out if a girl you've bound, gagged and raped is prepared to put a bullet in you?"

I suppose if Alex knew what she was doing with the gun, she would have pulled back the hammer as a way of punctuating her threat. Instead, she grips the gun with both hands and yells at the guy.

"Get your pervert ass in the house or I'm shooting you in the dick!" She lowers the gun and aims it at his crotch. At this, he moves, takes a few steps into the house, sets down his briefcase and puts his hands up. Kammie is crying, and I tell Alex to calm down.

I want to tell her that this shouldn't be about staying together anymore, that those are selfish thoughts, because even if Kammie is taken from us, foster care would be a better life than she's ever had. But I don't want to say it in front of Kammie, and I don't want to distract Alex, giving this guy a chance to grab the gun, and in one split second our freedom is gone.

I decide to play along, get the asshole to sit down and keep quiet while I get Alex calm enough to be rational about our options. Because if she can rip a man's throat out with her teeth, she can certainly pull a trigger.

"Toss your briefcase over there!" I say it loud, with authority.

"We're gonna want that, Stac."

"Why? What's in it?"

"Cuffs, a gag, an array of dildos to make up for his tiny prick. He's a real freak."

It makes all the sense in the world to cuff the guy, keep him restrained until we call the police. I'm hoping that's all Alex has in mind. I look around the room and see a wooden chair in the corner. "Sit in that chair!"

"No! In the kitchen, away from the windows." Alex grabs the chair and drags it toward the kitchen, the gun still on the guy.

I hug Kammie and tell her everything is okay and to go watch cartoons, that we're leaving soon. Reluctantly, she let's go, runs and grabs her fern and sits on the couch, rubbing the fern's leaves.

I head into the kitchen with the briefcase. The man is sitting in the center of the room in the chair. Alex is against the counter, gun aimed. I open the briefcase. Alex is right. Cuffs, a ball gag, and an assortment of rubber dildos of various sizes. Overkill.

"Put your hands behind the chair," she says.

He does, and I feed one cuff through the back of the chair and through another opening, then click a cuff over each wrist.

"Use the gag."

"I won't talk. I'll keep quiet," he says.

"Shut up, Steve! Use the gag, Stac. Let's see how he likes it."

I grab the gag and look it over. Thankfully, I've never seen one before, but I get the idea on how it works.

"I promise I won't say a word. I'll just sit here and do whatever you say."

I look at Alex. She's not letting up. "Open your mouth," she says.

"I promise . . . "

Alex grabs a pan from the sink and swings it at the guy's head. There's a loud thud and the man goes limp, and I have to stop the chair from tipping over.

"You didn't have to do that."

"Wake up, Stac. These guys deserve it." She helps me sit the guy upright in the chair. "Is it because you've only been here a year?"

"What do you mean?"

"Doc, this guy, the rest of them. They deserve everything coming to them, but it's like you have this . . . this empathy."

"It's not empathy. Personally, I hope they rot in prison where they're sodomized until they can't sit down, but I don't want their blood on my hands. I don't want to be a part of it, and I don't want Kammie to either. She can't handle this shit."

"I'm doing this *for* Kammie. So she knows she'll never have to be afraid again."

I can hear the volume on the TV go up as an ad for Kool-Aid comes on.

"This isn't the way to fix this, to be like them."

"Like them? We're not like them. Do you think the police will blame us for killing Doc? For tying up this asshole? They don't give a shit. They won't blame us one bit."

"Listen, I'll help you keep him here until we decide where we're going, but I'm not hurting him. And neither are you . . . .and once it's daylight, we're calling the police, then leaving."

"I can't go anywhere once the sun's up. You know that."

What I've been through the past year, it's been a living hell, and it was surprising how fast I'd given up hope, how fast it changed me. But Alex's anguish is on a whole other level. One completely separated from reality. Before, I just thought the whole vampire thing was her way of coping, becoming a part of the books she reads. Roleplaying in a way, like a kid in their bedroom strumming a broom handle along to music, the excitement and comfort of being someone else. But it's like she's stuck. This is what she believes. This is just her now.

CHAPTER 14

STACIA SQUINTED AS the flashes from the camera stirred her awake, just barely. To her, the light was nothing more than the sun coming up far too early, her eyes unwilling to cooperate after a night of mild drinking. Two shapes with deep voices moved in the room. As she struggled to focus, she recognized no one.

Her limbs were tugged and sheathed with socks, a shirt, pants, then left alone to drift away again as the flashing stopped and the room fell quiet. By the next day, when waking in the finished attic of a beachside house, she remembered none of it.

CHAPTER 15

ALEX SITS ON the counter and watches the guy drool onto his chest. A small amount of blood has colored his hair. It's not bad, but he'll wake up with a headache.

I join Kammie on the couch and hold her hand. The cartoons are too depressing to watch so I gaze out the window and watch the beach grass sway in front of the ocean. We could be anywhere along the coast, though I suspect we're still west.

I reach over and grab the Rolodex where Alex left it on a little table near the couch. On the table, there's a framed picture of a woman in a dress. Judging by the quality of the photo and the dress itself, the picture is several decades old, perhaps Doc's mother in her younger years. Maybe even grandmother. It's the only thing I've ever seen that shows Doc as being human.

I flip through the Rolodex, searching for addresses. I'm looking for a common city or state. California keeps popping up, but that could be family, keeping in contact after moving away. I tell Kammie that I'll be right back, and I go to look for mail. I head to Doc's office and find a piece right away. We're in Woodgrove

Beach, Oregon on Seaside Lane. Farther from home than I thought.

Home.

I go to the kitchen and tell Alex, but she already knows. She's got the guy's wallet in her hands, rummaging. She takes his money and flips through his pictures.

"Family man . . . Family *man*. You're such a man when you're putting up your Christmas lights, first on the block. Family man. Family *man*, I wanna crucify you to your front door, with nails from your well stocked garage, Family *man*."

She looks at me, sees the concern on my face. "Relax. It's a poem."

I'm still concerned.

"Well, we have money now." She holds up the bills.

"Good. Let's get the hell out of here."

"Not until tomorrow night."

"Do you have a plan? Anything at all? Something you can give me so I'm not sitting around wondering if you're gonna drink this guy's blood . . . or bait someone else here over the phone?"

"I didn't bring him here."

"No, but we weren't supposed to answer the door. That's what you said."

Alex says nothing. She knows she's in the wrong.

"You know I'm only still here because of you and Kam."

"I know."

"Come on, Alex. Give me something, will you?"

"What do you want me to say?"

"I don't want you to say anything. I want you to walk out that door with me and be done with this bullshit."

"I'm not letting them take her."

"You're being selfish."

"Behind closed doors, Stac."

I walk out of the kitchen and up to the front door, staring through the stained glass at a red-tinted world, knowing I should run. And knowing I won't.

CHAPTER 16

I'M EXHAUSTED. It's been a long night. And while we're usually up until noon, the adrenaline, the stress, it's caught up to me. I just want to be hidden away in a room filled with waterbeds and satin sheets, the glow of a TV and the nonsensical voices of TV personalities on low, keeping me company. Of course, Alex and Kammie would be there too, in their own comfy beds. And we'd wake to the smell of bacon and blueberry Pop-Tarts straight from the toaster, with not a care in the world.

I'm thankful for the TV here. It's kept Kammie entertained for hours. She's barely touched the fern since midnight. I know that means she's relaxed, completely distracted. Good.

Alex hasn't left the kitchen. She studies the Rolodex twice over and has a one-sided interrogation with the guy while he's knocked out. I spend time between the kitchen and the living room, keeping an eye on Alex, then sitting with Kammie for a while.

We find some cereal, and Kammie has her first bowl of Frosted Flakes. I think about baking cookies after seeing a box of mix in the cupboard, something to kill the time. That's all we're doing, killing time. Wasting time.

Again, I try to get Alex to leave. She says it's too close to daylight. Again, I ask her to consider letting the police handle everything, just pick up the phone and call. The call can even be anonymous. She isn't having it. She says we can't call until we're gone, yet she won't leave until tonight.

With our bedroom having only a single painted window, I'd never noticed her apprehension toward the sun. I wished I had. Maybe I could have talked sense into her before now.

The pacing and the cartoons and the arguing with Alex gets old. I need to get air, fresh air.

"I'm going for a walk," I say. "You should do the same, clear your head."

"I'm not leaving this guy by himself . . . Promise you won't go to the police?"

"If I was gonna do that I'd just pick up the phone."

"Okay . . . how's Kammie?"

"As well as she can be. She's still watching TV."

"Has she said anything?"

"Why would you ask that?"

"I don't know . . . I was just hoping that once we were free, maybe she'd talk again."

"We're not free."

"Tonight, okay? I Promise"

"Yeah . . . give me the money. I want Pop-Tarts."

Alex gives me a puzzled look.

"In case there's a store nearby."

"No police . . . you promised."

"Promise." It isn't a lie. And Alex was right, the damage that'd been done—Doc, this guy—we'd never get blamed for it. But just so long as it stops now.

She gives me the money—a handful of twenties, a

few tens and some ones—I kiss her on the cheek and whisper another promise so she doesn't worry. I go tell Kammie I'll be right back, then head out the front door. The one I don't remember coming through.

CHAPTER 17

Stacia woke disoriented. *This wasn't her room. A girl sat on the edge of the bed, holding her hand, caressing it. Her brow was bent to reflect concern, sympathy. Another girl sat at the end of the bed, her knees tucked under her chin.*

Panic-driven questions were asked. All were answered with tear-inducing revelation.

This was the first meeting of The Pale White.

CHAPTER 18

A FOOT OUT the front door and an ocean breeze hits me. It's like a hug, welcoming me back to the world. Instinctively, I close my eyes and breathe deep, letting it take me. I've never experienced euphoria before, but this is how I imagine it. My skin prickles with goosebumps and there's a smile on my face that feels like a crack in porcelain, something that doesn't belong. Thoughts of the past year and of the mess inside—the emotional trauma, the spilled blood—they steal the smile and rob me of anything that feels like happiness.

My eyes creep open and the moon screams hello as it paints the tips of beach grass and quiet waves. It's the most beautiful thing I've ever seen, but I can't enjoy it.

I look down and see a chair, there on the porch, a small table next to it with a book spread open. Doc's reading area. Doc's getaway. Where he sat and justified and watched the shore and enjoyed what he didn't deserve.

The house is at the end of a dead-end road, with the next house being at least a city block away. The windows are dark. They're either asleep or it's a vacation beach house and vacant most of the year. A convenience for Doc and his clientele.

I head down the porch steps and follow the road right. I can already see the glow of streetlights and shops somewhere down the road and around a bend. I want to run screaming toward them, announcing that I'm the girl who's gone missing. The one from California whose mother misplaced her in a drunken haze. The one who, as far as she can tell, was drugged, then sold, then . . .

But I made a promise. Actually, I'd made two. The other was to myself. A promise that once the sun fell again, I would leave. No matter what.

As I pass the driveway of Doc's house, I take note of the two vehicles in the driveway. Both new. Both very nice. Tinted windows, black. Made to be innocuous, yet red flags to any child who'd grown up with the mantra "Don't talk to strangers."

Despite the peace from the moon and waves, and the quiet whisper of beach grass, I can't help but feel paranoid. Scenarios play in my head of oncoming traffic recognizing me from behind blinding headlights and taking me back to the house and up into the attic, where we'd pay dearly for our escape for years to come. I would forever regret not calling the police when I had the chance.

I turn the bend, and the street ahead is a yellow tint that replaces the blue-gray hue of the moon. It's somehow more comforting, and I wish Kammie and Alex could see it. The rays of hope just ahead. It might change Alex's mind and we'd be on our way.

CHAPTER 19

EVERY SHOP ON the street is closed but one. As they should be. It's late. Or early. A convenience store beams brightly with neon lights advertising beer, cigarettes, and being open 24/7. It sits in a parking lot like a rectangular UFO, or more appropriately, an electric bug zapper, enticing the night owls to spend their money here.

It's discomforting to think Doc's operation is this close to civilization. Right under the noses of Woodgrove. The perverse demands and finishing grunts of monsters who belonged in prison nearly within earshot.

No one is in the store except for a single clerk. He sits behind the counter reading. Much like the ocean breeze, the chime above the door is another virtual hug, comforting in its familiar tone, announcing that I'm safe here.

It's brighter than daylight inside the store, and I squint my eyes. My skin looks translucent under the fluorescent lights. Like a vampire's skin might look. Now I'm glad Alex didn't come. She would use it to back her insane vampiric theory. She had already come up with an excuse as to why we can see her reflection. But the way the lights make me feel, make me look, she would run with it and try to convince me I'd been "turned" as well.

I find the candy aisle and grab some chocolate bars. A candy I know Kammie has never had. She's had suckers and gum before. We all got them from time to time. They were often part of the outfit.

I search the rest of the store and grab some orange soda, three bags of peanuts, three packages of donuts, microwaveable popcorn and an assortment of Little Debbie snack cakes. None of it healthy, but it's celebratory food. I want to share with Kammie everything she's been missing. Finally, I find the Pop-Tarts. Blueberry. I grab them as well as a half-gallon of ice cream and a package of chocolate chip cookies.

While at the counter, I add ropes of licorice to the pile of sweets. I will teach Kammie to bite off the ends and use it as a straw, turning the licorice gooey and somehow sweeter.

A sun glasses display catches my eye and I grab a pair, thick white frames. Next to it is an endcap of suntan lotion. I grab a bottle of what I think is the most protective and set everything on the counter. As the cashier bags everything up, he looks at me suspiciously, as though he recognizes me. I panic, grab the bags, drop two bills on the counter and run. I'm not even sure I've paid him enough.

"Hey!" he calls after me.

I exit the store and race down the road, taking a quick look behind me. The cashier is still in the store, behind the counter. I run faster and turn the bend, the groceries hitting my legs. Everything is far too loud out here in the quiet dark—my feet, the bouncing of the bags. I stop and catch my breath.

Once I get to the house, I take another look at the ocean, take another deep breath. It's cleansing, and my lungs no longer feel like they're filled with a year of homebound dust. Kammie greets me at the door. I think she's been watching for me. I smile big when I see her, remembering all the goodies I bought just for her.

"We're going to indulge," I tell her. She cocks her head at me like a confused pup.

I lead her to the kitchen, and when we pass the stairs I can smell Doc, the shit in his pants, the urine. It's subtle, but it's there. I don't think Kammie can smell it. She hasn't been outside, breathing the fresh air, cleansing her nose.

In the kitchen, Alex sits in the corner at the nook. She's made herself coffee and is writing in a notebook, the Rolodex next to her. The guy is still slumped in the chair, though now snoring. It's a comforting sound, knowing he's alive.

Alex looks up from the notebook. "Well? How was it? Were you scared?"

"A little." I don't tell her I ran from the store. I'm too excited to share everything I bought. "I come bearing gifts."

I set the bags on the counter and dig around for the sunglasses and sunscreen. "Close your eyes." While Alex has her eyes closed, I put the glasses and the sunscreen on the table in front of her. "Okay, open them."

She sees the sunglasses first and smiles. She puts them on immediately and starts striking mock poses.

"Do I look like a movie star? Or maybe a punk rock vixen on the run from Johnny Law?"

"They're you all the way." I tell her. "You look stunning. Sophisticated, yet angsty and adventurous."

At this she smiles, then sees the sunscreen. I watch her face put it all together, and I can tell that my good intentions aren't seen by her. There's a scowl, and she's silent for a moment, then takes the sunglasses off as though suddenly humiliated.

"Is this a joke?"

"I just thought it would help . . . protect you during the day." The words feel strange coming out, and I worry that I'm enabling, feeding the lie, the delusion. There's a fine line with this vampire bullshit, but these girls, they're fragile. We don't force Kammie to talk. We let her be who she needs to be to protect herself. Why should I try and tear down the wall Alex has built?

"This won't do anything. I walk out in the sun with this shit on and I'm toast . . . literally."

Her words remind me of a movie I'd seen once where a man defeated Dracula by tearing down a curtain, revealing the sun. Maybe I could do that when Alex isn't expecting it, prove to her she'll be fine, that she's not a vampire. None of us are. We're just screwed up in our own, different ways.

My hatred toward Doc and his clients swells. He's built Alex this self-imposed prison. Even when we're gone from this place, she still won't be free. She'll always be running, hiding. She'll always be afraid.

"I'm sorry, Al. I don't know the rules. I just thought it could help."

"Well, it won't. Mirrors are one thing. That's myth,

supernatural bullshit. This is science. The ultraviolet rays. It's real. Like salt on a slug."

"Okay. I'm sorry."

She goes back to writing in the notebook and Kammie tugs on my shirt, awaiting the goodies promised.

"I'm sorry, Kam. You're gonna love this. Remember in the book where the girl had ice cream and she dropped it and all the ants came and got fat and sticky?"

Kammie nods her head excitedly.

"Well, I got ice cream!"

I hand her the bucket of ice cream. She's never felt something so cold. There's such wonder in her eyes, such surprise at the cold against her skin, that for a moment I think—no, I hope—that she might speak, if only a few words, if only a single sound.

But she doesn't.

Alex has calmed down and watches as I empty the bags, then grabs three spoons and helps Kammie with the lid to the ice cream. Kammie digs in and gobbles a large bite.

"Careful, you eat that too quick and you'll get brain freeze. It'll burn, right here." Alex pinches the bridge of her nose between her eyes.

I sit down and grab a spoon. Alex looks at the counter and sees all the food. "I'm sorry, Stac. I know you were just trying." She touches my arm.

A phone rings in another room and time stands still. Ice cream drips, breaths are held. It rings four times before an answering machine picks it up.

"Hello, this is Jonathan Fields with Seaside Real Estate. If you'd like to make an appointment to see a

house, you can either reach me during office hours or leave a message and I'll call you back. Have a great day."

"Yeah, Doc. Kevin here. I'm canceling tonight. Something came up. Okay, catch ya tomorrow."

Jonathan Fields, Seaside Real Estate. I can see Alex already brainstorming with this new information.

"It's over, Al. Let it be. This isn't our fight anymore."

Alex starts to speak and the man in the chair stirs awake, lifts his head and moans. The three of us sit at the kitchen nook and watch him come to. The blood in his hair has dried, a line of it crusted on the side of his face. I feel nothing. If I'm completely honest, I find a small amount of pleasure in seeing him tied up and beaten into submission. It's a feeling that worries me, but how else should I feel? Empathy can only go so far. Do I want him dead? No, not by my hand. Or Alex's. Do I want him in prison? Forever.

He opens his eyes and they close again, like they're too heavy. He opens them again, squints. He's trying to focus, trying to make sense of what happened and where he is. He fixes on Alex with a blank stare, putting the pieces together while our bellies cool with burgundy cherry ice cream.

CHAPTER 20

"WHAT'S YOUR PLAN here, Alex?" the guy asks. I don't like that he uses her name. I can't explain why. It's like he doesn't deserve to.

Alex grins and it's a sinister thing with ill intent. "Well, *Steve*. If I had my way, you'd never leave this house alive."

"You're getting in deep girl. Kidnapping, assault . . . murder."

"I'm just getting started." She taps the notebook when she says it and I realize she's been matching names she knows with their addresses.

A killing spree.

"Come on . . . it can't be that bad here. Free room and board for you and your daughter."

"Shut up."

"It's like Doc's paying child support and you didn't even have to ask."

"I said shut up!"

"Alex, what does he mean, your daughter?"

"You're going to die, needledick!" Alex's eyes have gone wild, her mouth trembling. I can see the rage building within her.

"Alex . . . what does he mean?"

"Needledick? Now, you know better than that."

"Dude, shut the hell up . . . Alex, what is he talking about?"

"Wait . . . your friend here doesn't know?"

I'm confused and scared. Scared of what Alex might do. Doc was self-defense, but this. This would be different.

"Alex . . . ignore him. He's going to prison. He'll never be able to hurt you or anyone else, ever again."

"Prison?" the guy says. "I don't think so. I haven't done a thing wrong. I came here to visit a friend and was attacked by some crazy bitches I've never seen before."

Before I have a chance to hold her back, Alex jumps on the table, to the ground and across the kitchen. The spoons and the ice cream crash to the floor. Out of my periphery, I see Kammie cover her eyes as Alex tackles the man, and just like with Doc, buries her face into his neck.

The chair tips and Alex goes with it. The man screams and so do I. I scream for Alex to stop, but it's too late. I can see the pain in the man's face, the terror. His hands break free and he beats on her, claws at her. I climb over the table and try to reach them. Alex jumps back, her face painted red. She heaves and drops to the floor on her knees, unaware Steve has broken free. She heaves again and nothing comes up, not yet. I go for the pan Alex used earlier, but the guy kicks at my legs. My knees buckle and I go down. My ass hits the floor and my teeth clack. Pain shoots through my back and into my head. It's jarring, like being electrocuted—unexpected, shocking. My whole body feels it.

I don't even see the spoon in the guy's hand until the handle of it is plunged into Alex's chest. She grunts against the impact, falling flat on her back.

I'm screaming. Steve's screaming. He grabs his throat, gets up and runs toward the living room. Somehow, Alex stands up and gives chase. By this time, Steve is out the door, with Alex close behind. I begin to wonder if she'd really been stabbed. But as she runs through the doorway, I see her legs give and she disappears down the porch steps, tumbling. Before I run to the door, I get a quick look at Kammie. Her eyes are shut tight, her ears covered.

CHAPTER 21

ALEX RAN HER *finger across the stitches on her lower abdomen. They were like spider legs, a nest of them forcing their way out.*

"Can't have the baby damaging the goods." Doc had told her. "And no breastfeeding. I want your tits back to normal as soon as possible. Stretch Marks aren't exactly selling points."

But she had them anyway, subtle white lines along her hips. She loved them. She hated them.

Doc entered the room. He was thinner then, almost handsome, reeking of cologne. His breath held the stench of steak and beer.

"You'll start taking these." He threw a birth control dispenser on the bed. "One every day. Every. Single. Day. We can't have this happening again. You miss taking one and you'll go in the closet."

The closet. A cell meant for discipline. No light. No food. Just limited water, a bucket, and her own mind. Plenty of time to think. Too much time.

"If you're late on the rag, you tell me."

"Can I see her?"

"No . . . maybe in a few years. For now, you work

on that body of yours. Sit-ups, push-ups, whatever. Lose that gut on your own or I'll do it myself."

Doc shut the door, turned all four locks. Alex went back to fingering the spider legs and sang a lullaby, pretending her baby was still there.

CHAPTER 22

Wᴴᴱɴ ɪ ɢᴇᴛ out the door, Alex is sitting on the ground at the bottom of the steps, looking at the spoon sticking out of her chest. It's buried deep. So deep. I touch her arms and make her look at me. I'm crying. Inside I'm hysterical, but I'm trying to keep it together.

"Al, you're going to be okay." It feels like the biggest lie ever told.

She looks back at the spoon, touches it. "Silver."

"Don't touch it. I'm calling an ambulance."

She grabs my arm. "No!"

"You need help, Alex."

I don't even notice until he's speeding out of the driveway, that Steve has made it to his car. I didn't see his throat, but I saw the amount of blood, and if his wound is anything like Doc's, he's not getting very far.

"They'll take Kammie. Promise me you won't let them."

"We have to call someone."

"Promise me!"

Her voice is weak, and the blood around her mouth isn't just Steve's now. I look at the spoon jutting out of her. So very deep.

Then I see Alex smiling, staring out across the

ocean, and I notice a light in her eyes. The sun has split the horizon with a glowing orange line.

"I'm going to see the sun," she says. "It's . . . it's come to take me."

"Alex, please . . . you are not a . . . "

"Let it take me, Stac."

Kammie is standing on the porch, holding her fern, its leaves between her gently rubbing fingers. Her face is wet with tears, her eyes red.

"Kammie, bring me the phone." She disappears into the house, and I can't be sure she knows what a phone even looks like, but Alex has taught her so much. Taught her daughter so much.

"Please don't," Alex pleads. She coughs and blood sprays. "Take her with you and look after her."

Kammie shows up with the phone and I take it, but the look on Alex's face. The glow in her eyes brightens as the sun prepares to show itself.

"Watch with me." Alex pats the ground next to her. I sit and hold her, caressing her hair. But I'm not watching the sun. I'm watching Alex smile, the wonderment in her eyes as she sees the sun for the first time in years. The three of us sit on the ground and cry and hold one another as the sun takes Alex and sets her free.

And that was the end of The Pale White.

CHAPTER 23

I'M TORN BETWEEN wishing I'd called for help, and knowing Alex would have died either way. I'm torn between leaving her here or attempting a proper burial. But this isn't the wild west. You don't pick a lawn, dig a hole and stack rocks over a shallow grave.

Two things I know for sure. Alex would never want to be buried on this piece of shit's land, and the other, she'd want me to leave, now. Take Kammie and get the hell out of here.

I kiss Alex and tell her I love her. I grab Kammie and head inside. There is no time for a touching eulogy. No time for a moment of silence. It's daylight now, and Alex is slumped in the front of the house, covered in blood. And Steve, he's either dead in his car or getting help, maybe even sending the police. It will all trace back to Doc's, and we can't be here when it does.

I run upstairs and find Doc's bedroom. I search under his bed and in his closet and decide if I don't find a duffel bag, backpack, or some kind of luggage right away, then we'll leave without it. But I find a suitcase in his closet on the shelf. When I pull it down, I can tell it's not empty. I throw it on the bed and open it. Inside are manilla folders, pornographic magazines, and Polaroids—at least a dozen of them. Each polaroid has a name, date, weight and height written on it. The photos are of naked girls sprawled on beds. Their eyes are shut, sleeping. Drugged.

I scurry through them looking for mine. I find it, as well as one I think is Alex, but her hair is lighter. She's younger. Much younger. There is no picture of Kammie.

I empty the suitcase on the bed and put the pictures of me and Alex in a small pocket inside. I don't ever want anyone seeing them. I shut the thing and run downstairs. Kammie is sitting at the window, looking outside, looking at Alex. At her dead mother. The poor girl is the most fragile thing in the world right now, and I'm so afraid she'll break, that she'll never heal, never speak.

"Kam? I'm grabbing some food and we're leaving, okay?"

She slowly nods, wipes her face.

I head to the kitchen, and except for the ice cream, I put all the food I bought into the suitcase, including the orange soda and three bottles of water I find in the fridge. I picture us walking down the freeway, downcast and toting a suitcase and how suspicious we'll look. We can't go like that, not walking.

I look on every table for Doc's keys. I look for hooks near the door, in the kitchen, in his office and on his desk. Nothing. We need to get going. Where? I'm not sure yet. Just away from here. Away from the threat of losing Kammie, of breaking my promise.

Without giving myself time to think about it, I run upstairs, the stench of Doc's soiled pants growing stronger with every step. I head for the attic stairs. Doc's face is a gray-blue mask, bloated and clay-like. I search a pocket for the keys and my hands dampen with urine. I check the other pocket and find them. My eyes are drawn to his, and I freeze. I realize I've never looked into Doc's eyes before. I've always looked away, either out of intimidation or disgust. And now, two feet from his face, I study the milky things. The cloudy eyes of a soulless man. A bitterness stirs within me, and almost as a reflex, I spit on the monster's face. It does nothing for me. No healing takes place, no peace or contentment comes over me. But it's everything I ever wanted to say to him, but never could.

Before heading back downstairs, I fetch his wallet and take the $200 he won't be needing.

CHAPTER 24

I KNEEL BY Kammie at the window and take her hands in mine.

"Kam, listen to me. You know I love you and I'd do anything for you. Alex . . . she's not with us anymore, so I need you to trust me. We're leaving here, right now. We're going to take Doc's truck and leave. I have money and food. Remember all the goodies I got? We're bringing them and we're going to drive and eat and be free."

Her eyes are empty.

"What's been going on in this house will never, ever happen to you again. Okay?"

She nods and holds up her fern. I tell her of course she can bring it and whenever we get settled, she can have as many ferns as she wants.

"Hold it tight and grab onto me." I bend down and let her jump into my arm, straddling my side, her arms around my neck. She doesn't weigh nearly what she should. Neither of us do.

I stand at the threshold of the door and look at Alex, slouched like a marionette with its strings finally cut. We should have left right away. It's a regret I'll live with forever. With the suitcase in my hand and

Kammie in my arms, I take the stairs, being careful on the last step not to hit Alex. I place my hand on the back of Kammie's head and put her face in my hair. I don't want her to look.

I run to the truck and open the door for Kammie. Everything from here on out is new to her. While she has read books and seen pictures, and even heard stories from both Alex and I, I don't know exactly what will look familiar and what will look alien.

"Get in the seat, Kam."

She sets her fern on the floorboard and climbs into the truck. I try and buckle her up and tell her it's to keep her safe, but she doesn't want it. Either the idea of being restrained or the belt itself has triggered something. She grabs her fern and sits it on her lap, feels the leaves almost out of instinct, while her eyes are focused on the dashboard and all its knobs, switches and levers.

I run to the driver's side and listen for sirens, look for cars. It's clear. It's quiet. But it feels so wrong leaving the second Alex is dead, leaving her behind, and I need to keep reminding myself she would have it no other way. I can't even look at her again or I'll stop and never move, breaking every promise.

I climb in the truck and slide the key into the ignition. The engine turns easily. I throw it in reverse and expect to be blocked by a gang of men who just lost their menu on Seaside Lane. As we back out, I see Kammie look at her mother. Her chin quivers and she touches the glass.

This is goodbye.

CHAPTER 25

ONE STEP AT a time, I'm trying to form a plan. The first part being that we take Doc's truck as far as the train station, then dump it. By the time I'm standing in front of the ticket counter, I'm hoping to have the next step figured out. But for now, we drive.

It's hard to revel in the relief of being out of that house when the body of your best friend is in the rearview. And when small bursts of joy pop up, they're chased away by guilt. Guilt and worry. I've got Kammie to think about now. I've inherited this precious life I've no idea how to protect.

We're not even a mile away from the house, when I spot a commotion up ahead. It's Steve, the front of his car hugging a telephone pole. The car is surrounded by paramedics, police and bystanders, and as we sit at the light, I can see him, slumped over the wheel, soaked in blood.

I turn left to avoid the scene and watch my rearview obsessively until we're out of the area. I have no idea where I'm going but eventually find a freeway and head south. Despite her wet and swollen eyes, Kammie looks fascinated by everything around her. The other cars, the hilly terrain. But most of all, the people. When she sees them walking or driving in cars, it's hard to tell if she's afraid or curious.

"The world is full of good people, Kam. You'll see."

She looks at me, gives a half smile. There's a wall there, an unhealthy numbing. When Alex was killed there was no bawling, no freakout. Just simple tears and quiet grieving. And did she hear Steve? Does she understand who she is? Where she came from? Or did she already know?

As we drive, I tell her how special she is, about how much she's loved and her bright future ahead. I give her what I can to fight the pain inside, and I pray she understands.

CHAPTER 26

I STOP AT a gas station and ask a cashier if he'll write down directions to the nearest train or bus station. He asks another cashier and they talk about which one is closer and how to get there. Finally, they decide on the Oregon City Rail Station near Portland. They're not able to give me directions, but they have maps, so I buy one. Near the counter is a plush teddy bear holding a rose. I buy it too and head out to the truck.

I see a man pumping gas and he's staring at me. I probably wouldn't have recognized him at all, but there is this look on his face—a little worry, a little confusion. And I'm scared to death that he knows me.

He steps away from his car and out into the sun, and a spark of light on the side of his head reveals an earring I've seen before. A long, gaudy thing that has spent time hovering above my face, brushing against my neck.

I walk faster to the truck.

"Hey!" the man yells from behind. I ignore him and walk faster still. Kammie can see that I'm scared, and I hear the man's steps closing in on me. He runs behind the truck and cuts me off at the driver-side door.

"Where's Doc?" The man says it through gritted teeth, quiet but forceful.

"He's at the house."

"The hell you doin' with his truck?"

I look at Kammie. She's trembling, nostrils flared, and I can tell she's seen him before, too.

"I think you'd better come with me."

He barely gets the words out, when Kammie lunges at him through the window, her nails digging into his face, her mouth open and ready to bite. Just like her mother. And I wonder if she gets a hold of his throat will she rip it out. The man is shocked and slow to react, his face filled with reddening lines. He throws Kammie to the ground and reaches for his face, feeling the growing welts and shallow cuts.

Before he's done coddling his face, I kick him as hard as I can in the knee, and he drops to the pavement. I grab Kammie's hand and open the door. She climbs in. I'm right behind her. I can hear the man shouting as he clutches his leg. I start the truck and pull into the street. As I speed down the road, something I'd said to Kammie replays in my head.

The world is full of good people, Kam. You'll see.

It's salt in a gaping wound.

CHAPTER 27

KAMMIE IS NEAR hyperventilating, her hands shaking.

"Kam, I'm so sorry. That man back there . . . we just need to get out of here, out of this town, out of this state. Then you'll see the good people. The world is so big, much bigger than you know. And running into that guy back there . . . we're just too close to Doc's. That's all. Once we're on the train, you'll never see any of them again."

I teach her to breathe in through her nose and out through her mouth to catch her breath and relax. We do it together, and her breathing slows right away. I realize I still have the bag from the store clutched in my hand. I give Kammie the bear, and immediately she hugs it, gently brushing the fur with her hand. She sets the fern on the floorboard to make room for the bear on her lap. The bear has taken its place.

I've always thought she just had an appreciation for plants, particularly ferns—the feel of the leaves, or maybe the idea of caring for something and keeping it alive, helped her cope. It never occurred to me until now that it was just a desperate attempt at connecting with something. Anything. It was all she had. A plant.

No eyes to look into, no fur to caress, nothing to cuddle and accept her love. Nothing to love back. Yes, she had Alex. And later, me. But we were struggling, too. When you're just as lost, just as scared, it's impossible to carry the weight of another. To stay positive, to wear a smile that doesn't mean a thing. Kammie isn't stupid. She knew those smiles were plastic.

"I have more at my house," I say.

And then I realize that going home to my mother has always been the plan. Despite the alcohol. Despite James and his bachelor-pad decor, I need my mother. I have no choice.

We can't get to the train station fast enough. I want nothing to do with this truck. It belongs to a dead man, and recognizable by those who associate with him.

According to the cashiers, the station is nearly two hours away. I think of turning on the radio, something pleasant and relaxing I think Kammie might enjoy, then decide against it. I don't want her to be overwhelmed. I'm trying to look at the world through her eyes. I need to be careful. Instead of the radio, I sing to her. A familiar voice with familiar lyrics:

"And after all the feelings go, I see I still love you so.
I just thought I'd let you know now that everything's okay.
And you are on your way back, back to where you came.
She said with pain in her heart, it was there from the start.

Now I know why everything turns gray, but it's our own world we paint.

And I want the brightest. I want fluorescence, every day and night, for the rest of my life.
Open your eyes, won't you? Can't you see, you're so beautiful to me?"

I don't know what the song is or what it's about, but I've heard Alex sing it countless times, and Kammie always seemed to enjoy it. Maybe not the most appropriate song, but like I said: Familiar voice, familiar lyrics.

I can tell Kammie is tired—trading sleep for scenery. For the entire drive, I struggle back and forth with just heading to the police. It seems inevitable anyway. But I keep picturing Kammie in the back of a police car, by herself, waiting to be questioned, examined, interrogated and ultimately caged, waiting for life to begin and unsure of what comes next, with no one there who can relate. No one she can trust.

My concerns feel tedious—a monotonous battle with making the right decisions. And if I don't buckle down and think straight, it'll only make things harder. I make up my mind that every decision I make from here on out is a good one, with our best interest in mind, always. No more second guessing. No more guilt. No more questioning.

CHAPTER 28

Aɴ ʜᴏᴜʀ ɪɴᴛᴏ our trip and Kammie is finally asleep, crashed from the adrenaline that's kept us going. I've got one eye on the road ahead, the other behind, looking for police. I drive the speed limit. Exactly. I finally put the radio on, low, and use the music for distraction. But my mind wanders anyway, bouncing from one anxious thought to another. Seeing my mother for the first time in a year, the blood-spattered house on Seaside Lane, the first person to find Alex and what it may do to them. Will it be a friendly local out for a morning jog? Or one of Doc's clients, a wallet full of money toward a young piece of taboo ass? I hope for the latter. That the image of Alex's lifeless body will forever haunt the predator until his last painful breath.

I stop at a rest area and wake Kammie. We both use the restroom and I break out the Pop-Tarts, and we eat them there in the truck. Kammie seems to enjoy them, and I tell her how much better they are toasted. I explain how a toaster works, and she listens intently. It helps us to forget.

A family of four parks next to us. They stretch their legs and use the bathroom. I can tell they're on vacation. They're full of excitement and chatter, about how they can't wait to get to Disneyland. The husband complains that maybe they should have flown, and the wife goes on about the advantages of driving there: Sightseeing, quality time together, hotels, restaurants. The interaction is the closest thing to normalcy Kammie has ever seen.

I take the time to explain where they're going and that maybe one day we can go, too. But I don't promise it. The promises I've made already feel impossible to keep, and I want Kammie to trust me, to feel safe. Always.

We finish our food and watch the family prepare a picnic in the grass. The two kids play while their parents lay out a blanket and pull food from a wicker basket. One of the boys looks to be Kammie's age, and I can see her watching him, curiously, as he plays with his younger sister.

Kammie finds a pen in the cupholder between the seats. She takes the map and begins writing on the cover of it. Alex taught her to write, and by the time I was in the house, Kammie could write simple sentences. But she doesn't write them often. And if we push her, she gets agitated and even more distant.

She takes her time writing, focusing hard on each letter, then hands me the map and watches me closely. I fight back tears while reading the words:

"Do we need blud? If do. I want boy."

CHAPTER 29

DESPITE DOING MY best to hold back, tears spill, and I quickly brush them away. Kammie reaches over and caresses my arm, then hands me her bear. I cry harder. The idea that Kammie is a danger to anyone just kills me. But I have to be real. Just me loving her won't end her suffering. It won't heal the scars. It won't stop potential mental illness or PTSD or depression. I can worry and coddle and act as a safety net for Kammie, but when the damage has been done, it feels like a waiting game. Will she ever speak again? Will she ever be able to love a man and start a family? Will she one day mask the pain with substance abuse?

Will she kill?

I wipe my tears and turn to face her. Her eyes are large and wondering, worried and confused.

"Kammie . . . we do not need blood. We will *never* need blood. We need food and water and sleep and sunlight. We need good people. Honest, trustworthy, and loving people."

As I say the words, I feel like I'm up against everything Alex has taught her, whether directly or indirectly. Kids are smart. They pick up on everything. They mimic, whether bad or good. They watch, they listen, and they learn. And before they're even old enough to question anything, they act.

There are the outliers, like those who grow up in alcoholic homes and run the other way rather than following the same path. My plan is to be one of them. But it feels like a roll of the dice with each life.

"Blood is . . . it's what got Alex killed. Her way of thinking? That's Doc's fault. He messed her thinking up. But you and I . . . we need to be strong and not let him ruin us." I don't know how deep I can go without Kammie tuning out. "I'm going to show you how life is supposed to be, but in the meantime, you've got to try and block out all the bad. Okay?"

She nods her head and it's a weight lifted. I give her back the bear, tell her I love her so much and kiss her head. And as we drive away from the rest stop, I see her watching the boy. And I hope and pray that her thoughts are on their happiness, and not their blood.

CHAPTER 30

WHEN WE GET to Oregon City, I feel so much
lighter. We're nearly two hours away from Woodgrove
and close to dumping the truck. I stop at a gas station
for more specific directions. The gas tank is closing in
on E, but I don't get gas. No sense in it.

I ask Kammie if she wants to go inside with me and
she nods. I can tell she's nervous. This will be her first
time in public. I hold her hand and we walk in. There's
a lot for her virgin eyes to see. Colorful displays,
coolers filled with drinks and ice cream, magazines
and people.

An older man walks by us and winks at her, smiles.
She grabs me tight and plants her face in my side. The
man chuckles and thinks it's cute.

We wait in a short line in front of the counter and
Kammie keeps close to me, no longer interested in her
surroundings. I ask the cashier for directions and am
surprised to find we're nearly there, so I decide to
drive the truck another few miles and park it on a side
street.

I find a neighborhood to park the truck, a newly-
paved road with wide lanes. Wide enough to park the
truck without obstructing traffic and raising suspicion.

Kammie leaves her fern in the truck—it's not needed anymore—and we start walking.

Kammie and I share a water as we walk, and I wish the suitcase were a backpack or duffel bag, or even a grocery bag. Something that doesn't announce to the world that we're two runaways fleeing the state. It also makes us look desperate and vulnerable—targets for the kind of assholes we're running from in the first place.

Kammie goes back to taking in the sights, showing a profound interest in such simple things that we all take for granted. Pointing at manicured bushes on front lawns, fire hydrants, a barking dog through a chain-link fence. With each point of her finger, I give explanation—a short, detailed lesson on each.

If anything can help keep her distracted while healing takes place, it's exploring a brand-new world. But it's the night I truly worry about. As we acclimate to a normal day/night schedule and she lies in bed in a darkened room, her eyes fixed on the ceiling. When the dark takes advantage of weak minds, tapping you on the shoulder, reminding you of your sins, and those who've sinned against you. When sleep won't come and there's too much time to think. Those are the moments I fear. For the both of us.

CHAPTER 31

WE'RE AT THE train station, and the closer we get to truly being free, the more anxious I feel. Two hours away from Woodgrove, yet I feel like we're just now running out the front door on Seaside Lane, waiting to be stopped and pulled back in. Letting the world know right now everything that happened back there feels so much easier. Telling at least one person. Until then, I'm not sure I'll truly feel safe.

As I give our destination to the woman at the counter, I grow concerned about money. I've never bought a plane, bus, or train ticket before and have no idea what to expect. She punches the keys on her keyboard and I'm holding my breath. Inside I'm on fire, running down the street screaming for help, wanting to go back in time. I want to jump into those baby pictures and be held tight by a mother whose breath smells of protection and tenderness— not of a poisoned liver and ashtray tongue. Whose touch feels like love and devotion—not cold and distant.

"Cash or charge?" the woman asks, and it breaks the bubble of panic I'm suffocating in.

"Cash."

Then she gives me the price, and I know I have enough. Thank God I have enough.

I give the woman the money. Exact change. She hands me the tickets and says, "The train departs at 2:30." I look at the clock on the wall behind her. We have three hours. An eternity.

CHAPTER 32

Kammie and I sit in the grass in the shade of a tree behind the station and drink the orange soda through licorice straws. I tell her where we're headed. She knows all about my mother and James and I tell her not to worry, that we'll feel it out, and if things aren't safe or comfortable, we'll be out of there. I still have plenty of money left, plus I'd saved a little from babysitting. It's hidden in my bedroom. It may not get us far but it's something. It's a start.

We lie here in the shade and I point out faces and animals in the clouds and make up stories about them. Kammie snuggles up next to me and we both doze off, in and out of sleep—the occasional horn or car door startling us awake, giving us brief glimpses of the bright blue sky before we doze again. It's a beautiful sky and I hope Kammie can appreciate it, because I can't. Not yet.

CHAPTER 33

WE'RE STIRRED AWAKE a final time by the incoming train. We watch the people get off, then stand in line to board. Kammie's hand is clammy in mine. I tell her how peaceful trains are and how we can even walk around while it's moving. I've never been on one before, but the distant sound of them from my bedroom window has always been pleasant to me, and I imagined being a part of that sound would be even better.

Kammie nervously rubs her thumb across mine, and I keep talking to relax her. I poke fun at an old lady's hat and how big it is and how she'll need two seats by herself just to have room for it. Kammie gives a voiceless giggle that feels more for my benefit than anything, then it's our turn to board for the eight-hour ride to Jexton.

We walk up the steps and are led to our seats by a very kind man who reminds me of a math teacher I had in high school, Mr. Artwell. He used to stand near the door while the students came in, and he always had something nice to say when he saw you. "Nice shoes you've got there. I'll bet you can run a mile in under seven minutes in those babies" or "I'm glad to see you're feeling better today. Class isn't the same without you." A pleasant greeting for each and every student. And when he moved to Louisiana, some students even cried. I was one of them. I used to think that if my dad were still alive, he might be a lot like Mr. Artwell.

I give Kammie the window seat so she can watch the scenery ahead and maybe feel safer away from the aisle. I slide the suitcase under our seat and find a magazine there. I grab it. It's a parenting magazine with a baby on the cover, smiling with big, beautiful eyes. We thumb through the magazine and she points to her favorite pictures, mostly ones with babies sleeping peacefully or being held, or any picture with a stuffed animal in it.

Finally, the train leaves Oregon City and I say "good riddance" for the both of us. I hand her the magazine and tell her I'm going to try and sleep, and when I wake we'll try the cookies I bought. Kammie holds her bear and carefully brushes away any hair that may be touching its black marble eyes.

It doesn't take long before the train lulls me to sleep, where I dream of keeping Kammie in a cage in my bedroom closet and feed her like a pet. One bowl filled with cookies and ice cream. The other with blood. And in my dream, I keep telling myself this is all for the best.

CHAPTER 34

THREE HOURS GO by and I wake in a panic. I reach for Kammie. She's right next to me, asleep. I think about the dream I had and wonder if it meant something, and I find myself doing exactly what I said I wouldn't do. Questioning everything. Am I being selfish? Is this really for the best? Did the dream mean anything at all, or was it just a senseless nightmare brought on by trauma?

The bear is wrapped in Kammie's arms, the magazine open on her lap and turned to a page with the picture of a new mother holding her precious child—the picture Kammie looked at the most—I'm convinced she knows who her mother was. Or that she longs for one.

I stand to stretch my arms and legs and look at the people around me. I smile at those who make eye contact and count the smiles. My way of looking for hope in mankind, something I've asked Kammie to do while struggling myself.

Three smiles. I'll take it.

I sit back down and Kammie wakes up. She grips her bear tighter and smiles at me through a sleep-swollen face.

"We're halfway there, girl. Wanna go for a walk?"

She nods. I grab our cookies, and we head through the car and into the next one where there's a bar with refreshments and all the seats face the windows. We sit and watch the trees race by in a beautiful green blur, and I tell Kammie about the crabapple tree in my backyard and how we can climb it and sit on the branches and eat cookies and watch the birds.

The green blur gives way to an open field as far as our eyes can see, and I imagine to Kammie it must look like a golden ocean, the wind swaying the wheat like the waves she'd watch from the attic window on Seaside Lane.

I get us each a milk from the bar, and we sit quietly and eat all the cookies, watching the distance between our old life and new one grow further apart.

CHAPTER 35

EVENTUALLY, WE END up back in our seats, and every time the train makes a stop, my stomach cramps with a whole different type of fear. The fear of going home. The fear of being disappointed, of disappointing Kammie.

With the conversation being one-sided, I have a hard time staying awake. We're usually long in bed at this time—the best part of each day for the past year, the quiet escape of slumber, where we prayed for dreams that took us away, even if only for a short while.

Kammie and I both give in to another nap and the next time we wake it's from a voice calling out that we've arrived in Jexton.

CHAPTER 36

As WE STEP off the train, I'm no longer afraid of being recognized by any of Doc's people. It's the locals I may know that I'm afraid of, or even the people who've stared with sad eyes at my face on the local news, in the newspaper, or on telephone poles and store windows.

Missing: Stacia Ann Squires, 5' 7", 120 lbs (though closer to 110 now)*, blue eyes. Last seen wearing . . .* would my mother even know? Or worse yet, did my mother even bother to report me missing? Or did she write me off as a runaway, her better judgment swayed by the manipulative ways of James? This starts to feel like crawling back. And when I get there, I'll wish I never showed my face.

I can see James at the door, greeting me: *"Got tired of tryin' to make it on your own, huh? Maybe now you'll appreciate what your mother and I do for you. Now clean up the kitchen and earn your way."*

We're about two miles from my house. I don't want to lug the suitcase around anymore, so we go to a convenience store and I ask for a bag and buy a baseball hat with palm trees on it. It's ugly and doesn't fit well, but I get it to tuck my hair and hide my face.

Being recognized would bring too many questions, and ultimately the police.

I take the rest of our food and water out of the suitcase and put it in the bag, even the microwave popcorn that we may never be able to eat. I take the Polaroids and put them in my pocket without Kammie seeing, then ditch the suitcase in some bushes and head toward the falling sun. Toward home.

CHAPTER 37

It's SURREAL WALKING home, passing the high school where I should be graduating. The brick building holds no good memories. It's just another place I sat and felt alone, disconnected. The kids inside running their own kingdom filled with divided tribes who don't speak the same language yet eat the same food, share the same chairs, and walk the same halls.

I recall my first night at Doc's, lying there in a strange bed, wishing that the next day I could be in that lonely brick building. A place I despised, with people I didn't like. I longed for it deeply. Even if that very next day I found myself in the girl's locker room surrounded by snickering whispers of tiny breasts and a flat ass. I welcomed it. I prayed for it.

And yet as I pass by the building now, there is no sigh of relief that I've made it. No half smile. My freedom wasn't supposed to be like this, lugging a frightened, mute child into my own hell filled with dysfunction and alcohol, and yet another male figure to taint her image of men forever.

I squeeze Kammie's hand and she squeezes back. The most she's ever really said to me. But I know that it means, "I love you."

CHAPTER 38

I TELL KAMMIE that we're almost there and that I can't be sure how this will go down, but no matter what, every day of her life from here on out will be the best she's ever had. I don't think she really understands what I mean. And even though I'm scared for her, I'm more excited than anything.

As we turn onto my street, I can see the silhouette of my house looming like a giant beast ready to devour all hope. The street is dark, except for a single street light that's normally burned out, mostly from neighborhood kids throwing rocks at it. When I was younger, I liked the dark and mysterious way the houses looked while the light was gone, like shuttered Jack o' lanterns all in a row. But as I grew older and the street light failed to cast its glow, it made me feel insecure and forgotten and insignificant, and the street became a den of thieves where bikes were stolen and houses vandalized under a merciless black sky. But still, as beautiful as the ocean view on Seaside Lane was, it's nothing compared to the familiarity of home, warts and all.

The cramps in my stomach turn to nausea as Kammie and I walk down the street, my house a stone's throw away. The lights are on and the curtains in the bay window are drawn, giving a full view of the living room.

As we get closer, it doesn't look like my house at all. It's the same dirty white, the same roof with missing shingles, and even the same welcome mat with the faded green letters. But there are flowers planted along the walk, surrounded by mulch, and the weeds along the house have been pulled, the grass neatly trimmed. Care has been taken here.

I look through the window. The tapestries and posters of eagles, motorcycles, skulls, and women have been replaced by fresh paint and framed pictures of landscapes and painted flowers.

There's lead in my gut as I realize my mother has moved. A house I spent my entire life in now belongs to someone else. Someone who the neighbors no doubt rejoice over daily with the loss of the scourge that once lived here.

Kammie feels me crying and squeezes my hand. I don't squeeze back because it doesn't really register. She squeezes again, touches my arm and caresses it, then offers me her bear once more.

There was never a plan B. In my head, I was making it work somehow, without even thinking it through. I guess I thought my desire, my need, would be enough for a miracle and maybe my mother would try and help, put down the bottle long enough to think of me for a change, maybe even James, too.

I pull the money from my pocket and count it. There should be enough for at least a few nights in a shitty motel and more food, but real food. Not cookies and candy, ice cream and soda. I'll start right away on getting a job, even some shit job at a fast food joint, anything to keep us afloat.

Now to explain to Kammie that I have no idea what the hell we're doing. When I look at her I smile, and it's a legitimate smile because I know that even sleeping under the stars tonight is better than sleeping under the oppressive blanket that is Doc's house and its many demons.

Movement in the window catches my eye. It's a woman. She's vacuuming, her back to us. And for a moment I let myself believe it's my mother, preparing the house for my welcoming home. But her figure is not frail and cachectic. Her hair isn't thrown into a messy ponytail, too lazy for anything else. But her movements. They're familiar.

I creep onto the lawn, pulling Kammie with me, and watch the woman. While the decor in the house has changed, most of the furniture has not. The bookshelf holds the same books, but they're organized, not haphazardly set in chaotic stacks among ashtrays and empty bottles.

This is my mother cleaning. This is her twenty pounds heavier. This is the beautiful woman in the baby pictures.

CHAPTER 39

I RUN TO the front door and knock. It's a timid knock, frightened and insecure. I can still hear the vacuum. She hasn't heard me. Should I just walk in? This is my home.

My home.

I knock again, louder, and the vacuum turns off. My hands are shaking, my mouth dry. The door opens with the familiar sound of rubber seal on metal frame. The look on my mother's face I know I'll keep forever, and it somehow makes up for the years of neglect. It's a still picture I can call on during trying times, like an old song that brings back better days.

There's a scream of surprise and joy as my mother's face contorts into a ball of trembling wrinkles, her hands frantically working the latch to the screen door. I've never seen another person hug and hold someone the way she does me. It's full of love, relief, and apologies. My absence has crushed her.

She trembles in my arms, sobbing uncontrollably and smelling of shampoo and perfume. Not of cigarettes. Not of alcohol. In this moment it's so easy to forgive. So damn easy.

Kammie holds me too, pushing her face against me

and adding to the trembling mess of tears and joy. It's the hardest I've seen her cry before, and I swear I can almost hear it.

After we finally release, my mother invites us in, demands it. She's manic in her actions and voice, repeatedly asking if we're hungry, if there's anything we need, and what on earth happened to me.

The house is near unrecognizable, both by appearance and by scent. My mom can't sit still, can't stop shaking and smiling and crying. It's the welcoming I'd hoped for, prayed for, but never really expected. Out of all the frantic gabbing, my mother's biggest concern is where have I been? What happened?

Eventually, the right words come. And as I speak them, my mother falls apart. She's hugging me and gasping and sobbing, and I can tell she blames herself. Through all the explaining, I tell her about Alex and Kammie and the men who died. She asks no questions. She just listens, and with eyes staring right into mine, she gives me all the attention she possibly can. The tears I shed are both from reliving the last twenty-four hours and seeing the mother I've always wanted but never had.

She hugs Kammie, too. Kissing her, crying for her, and damning every man who did this to her. I leave out the part about Alex being her mother because I still can't be sure Kammie understands. It'll come up one day, when she's ready, and maybe even from her own mouth.

We talk for hours and it's so very surreal. The listening ear, the advice, the empathy my mother holds, the instant love she has for Kammie. And while it all feels too good to be true, I take it all in. Every bit of it. Because this isn't a dream. I will not be waking up in a room on Seaside Lane. I'll be waking up in Jexton.

Mom makes us a midnight meal of blueberry pancakes. I pour us all big glasses of milk, and while I'm in the fridge I take note that there is no alcohol. No beer, no vodka, not even wine. The change in the house, my mother's appearance, and now the lack of drink, feels like an elephant in the room, something either purposely being avoided or just not the right time. But I bring it up. I've got to know.

"Mom . . . where's all the alcohol?"

She pauses, and her eyes well up, which seems impossible given the amount she's already cried tonight.

"I'm not that person anymore, honey . . . and I'm so sorry it took what it did for me to wake up. I know I've hurt you . . . but I promise . . . "

"It's okay, Mom."

She puts her hand on mine and her chin quivers under the weight of guilt and the power of being forgiven. The abstinence from alcohol is not a new thing for her, I can tell. There is too much growth here, my disappearance being the catalyst for the change to take place. This isn't a phase. This is a lifestyle. This is her now.

"And James?"

"I kicked that piece of shit out nearly a year ago. It's just you and me now." She looks at Kammie and smiles. "And this precious one."

We talk openly about contacting the police in the morning and telling them everything. Mom says that in a perfect world the police would come, hear what we have to say, then leave us be, including Kammie. But she says this isn't a perfect world, so that's not what will happen.

"You know, the worst-case scenario here is that you don't see Kammie every day, just for a while. That's all. They don't lock these kids away behind bars, away from the public. And if I had to make a guess, I'd say she'd only have a temporary vacation from this old house before she came right back here for good. There's a history between you two. One that will be considered."

Then Mom drops a few names, both of which are affiliated with the very system I'm so afraid of Kammie entering. Both of whom are dear friends of Mom. New friends who've only seen the new her. And she tells me that while Kammie may not be able to avoid the system altogether, that Mom will be doing everything in her power to provide a safe and loving home for her, right here at the house.

She seems optimistic, and after we talk I can tell Kammie understands, and there's a smile on her face that doesn't seem to be able to leave.

Kammie and I head for bed and Mom doesn't want to leave us, so she grabs a blanket and sits in the chair in the corner of my room. Kammie marvels at all the stuffed animals on my bed. I tell her she can sleep with whichever ones she wants. She seems to love them all but chooses the bear I bought her.

We hit the lights and Mom says a prayer for us, asking God to protect us and thanking Him for setting us free, and her free, too.

With bellies full of blueberry pancakes, Kammie

and I hold hands and close our eyes. We're okay now. We're free. I kiss her forehead and whisper in her ear goodnight. And just before I slip into the best night's sleep I've had in years, she whispers it back.

ABOUT THE AUTHOR

Chad has written for Famous Monsters of Filmland, Rue Morgue, Cemetery Dance, and Scream magazine. He's had a few dozen stories published, and some of his books include: *Of Foster Homes & Flies*, *Wallflower*, *Stirring the Sheets*, *Skullface Boy*, and *The Same Deep Water as You*. Lutzke's work has been praised by authors Jack Ketchum, Stephen Graham Jones, James Newman, Cemetery Dance, and his own mother. He can be found lurking the internet at www.chadlutzke.com.

THE END?

Not if you want to dive into more of Crystal Lake Publishing's Tales from the Darkest Depths!

Check out our amazing website and online store or download our latest catalog here.
https://geni.us/CLPCatalog

Looking for award-winning Dark Fiction?
Download our latest catalog.

Includes our anthologies, novels, novellas, collections, poetry, non-fiction, and specialty projects.

Where Stories Come Alive!

We always have great new projects and content on the website to dive into, as well as a newsletter, behind the scenes options, social media platforms, our own dark fiction shared-world series and our very own webstore. Our webstore even has categories specifically for KU books, non-fiction, anthologies, and of course more novels and novellas.

Readers. . .

Thank you for reading *The Pale White*. We hope you enjoyed this novella.

If you have a moment, please review The Pale White at the store where you bought it.

Help other readers by telling them why you enjoyed this book. No need to write an in-depth discussion. Even a single sentence will be greatly appreciated. Reviews go a long way to helping a book sell, and is great for an author's career. It'll also help us to continue publishing quality books.

Thank you again for taking the time to journey with Crystal Lake Publishing.

Visit our Linktree page for a list of our social media platforms. https://linktr.ee/CrystalLakePublishing

Follow us on Amazon:

MISSION STATEMENT:

Since its founding in August 2012, Crystal Lake has quickly become one of the world's leading publishers of Dark Fiction and Horror books. In 2023, Crystal Lake officially transitioned into an entertainment company, joining several other divisions, genres, and imprints, including Torrid Waters, Crystal Lake Comics, Crystal Lake Games, Crystal Lake Kids, and many more.

While we strive to present only the highest quality fiction and entertainment, we also endeavour to support authors along their writing journey. We offer our time and experience in non-fiction projects, as well as author mentoring and services, at competitive prices.

With several Bram Stoker Award wins and many other wins and nominations (including the HWA's Specialty Press Award), Crystal Lake Publishing puts integrity, honor, and respect at the forefront of our publishing operations.

We strive for each book and outreach program we spearhead to not only entertain and touch or comment on issues that affect our readers, but also to strengthen and support the Dark Fiction field and its authors.

Not only do we find and publish authors we believe are destined for greatness, but we strive to work with men and women who endeavour to be decent human beings who care more for others than themselves, while still being hard working, driven, and passionate artists and storytellers.

Crystal Lake Publishing is and will always be a beacon of what passion and dedication, combined with overwhelming teamwork and respect, can accomplish. We endeavour to know each and every one of our readers, while building personal relationships with our authors, reviewers, bloggers, podcasters, bookstores, and libraries.

We will be as trustworthy, forthright, and transparent as any business can be, while also keeping most of the headaches away from our authors, since it's our job to solve the problems so they can stay in a creative mind. Which of course also means paying our authors.

We do not just publish books, we present to you worlds within your world, doors within your mind, from talented authors who sacrifice so much for a moment of your time.

There are some amazing small presses out there, and through collaboration and open forums we will continue to support other presses in the goal of helping authors and showing the world what quality small presses are capable of accomplishing. No one wins when a small press goes down, so we will always be there to support hardworking, legitimate presses and their authors. We don't see Crystal Lake as the best press out there, but we will always strive to be the best, strive to be the most interactive and grateful, and even blessed press around. No matter what happens over time, we will also take our mission very seriously while appreciating where we are and enjoying the journey.

What do we offer our authors that they can't do for themselves through self-publishing?

We are big supporters of self-publishing (especially hybrid publishing), if done with care, patience, and planning. However, not every author has the time or inclination to do market research, advertise, and set up book launch strategies. Although a lot of authors are successful in doing it all, strong small presses will always be there for the authors who just want to do what they do best: write.

What we offer is experience, industry knowledge, contacts and trust built up over years. And due to our strong brand and trusting fanbase, every Crystal Lake Publishing book comes with weight of respect. In time our fans begin to trust our judgment and will try a new author purely based on our support of said author.

With each launch we strive to fine-tune our approach, learn from our mistakes, and increase our reach. We continue to assure our authors that we're here for them and that we'll carry the weight of the launch and dealing with third parties while they focus on their strengths—be it writing, interviews, blogs, signings, etc.

We also offer several mentoring packages to authors that include knowledge and skills they can use in both traditional and self-publishing endeavours.

We look forward to launching many new careers.

This is what we believe in. What we stand for. This will be our legacy.

Welcome to Crystal Lake Publishing— Where stories come alive!

www.ingramcontent.com/pod-product-compliance
Lightning Source LLC
Chambersburg PA
CBHW070911100726
47907CB00008B/2283